Meet the Characterz

Melvin Meadly

Daisy

DI Meadly

Priti Kaur

Vampire mite

Worker 50

Mr Johnson

Mr Jolly

Norman Crudwell

Before you read
Curse of the Vampire Mites
I want to remind you why bees
are so important . . .

It's not just because they give us honey.
Bees and other insects

pollinate

the plants that keep our world alive.
No pollination – NO PLANET!

Pollination is an important part of the life cycle of plants. Pollen must be carried between flowering plants to fertilize them so they can make seeds that will grow into new plants.

POLLEN

And this is where bees help. When a bee feeds on nectar from flowers (nectar is the sweet sticky stuff that bees turn into honey), pollen on the flower sticks to the bee's body and gets transported to other flowers. As the bee buzzes from plant to plant it is pollinating the flowers!

POLLEN

For George Pattison – an avid
reader of the Bee Boy books!

OXFORD
UNIVERSITY PRESS

Great Clarendon Street, Oxford OX2 6DP

Oxford University Press is a department of the University of Oxford.
It furthers the University's objective of excellence in research, scholarship, and
education by publishing worldwide. Oxford is a registered trade mark of Oxford
University Press in the UK and in certain other countries

The moral rights of the author/illustrator have been asserted
Database right Oxford University Press (maker)

First published 2019

British Library Cataloguing in Publication Data

Data available

ISBN: 978-0-19-276391-4

1 3 5 7 9 10 8 6 4 2

Printed in China

Paper used in the production of this book is a natural,
recyclable product made from wood grown in sustainable forests.
The manufacturing process conforms to the environmental
regulations of the country of origin.

BEE BOY

Curse of the Vampire Mites

Tony De Saulles

OXFORD
UNIVERSITY PRESS

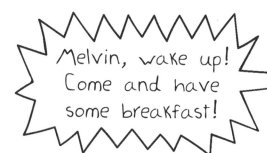

Melvin, wake up! Come and have some breakfast!

Eh? Huh? Oh no, I've been dreaming again. Trouble is, the nightmare's not over. My bees are OK on the roof of Meadow Tower, but in other places bees are dying out fast. Scientists call it The Great Pollination Pickle. Bees need flowers but with more people in the world, farmers have to grow crops where wild flower meadows used to be and the chemicals used to control pests and weeds can sometimes harm bees . . .

HURRY UP, LOVE!

. . . and that's not the worst thing – all over the planet, plagues of vampire mites are infesting hives, feasting on bees' blood and spreading disease. Our pollinators really are in trouble and people are only just starting to realize. No pollination will mean no apples, onions, cabbages, coconuts, or . . . well, the list is a mile long. We MUST look after our bees. I'M WORRIED!

Bleary-eyed, I wander into the kitchen. It's Wednesday morning.

Mum hands me a plate. 'Toast?'

'Can I have honey?'

Mum's firm: 'No. You've eaten this week's ration.'

'Aw, Mum! I'm a bee-keeper,' I groan. 'I should have honey whenever I want!'

'I know, love. But fruit and veg costs a fortune, and now the price of meat is shooting up too,' Mum explains in her usual kind, calm way.

'Until the Pollination Pickle
is solved, we need to be
careful with our food
supplies. Honey is precious
stuff – it's fifty pounds
a jar in the shops!'

I nod, feeling sorry for my whinging.
'OK, Mum. I know we're in trouble –
humans, I mean. I'm doing my best to
tell everybody how important bees are,
but they don't always listen.'

Mum ruffles my hair.
'Cheer up, love,
at least you're
trying!'

Starting the Bee Club was my idea. We meet once a month, in the school library. Mrs Gashkori, our librarian, clears one of the big round tables and lends us a flipchart if we need it. The club's not just for children — Mrs Gashkori, Miss Springfield, and Mrs Bottomly have all become bee-keepers since we started.

Being in charge was scary at first, but I've already got seven members and it's like Priti says, 'Only people who really care about bees are allowed in, so I don't need to be nervous.'

Here we are again, ready for our chat.

'Thank you all for coming,' I say. 'I'm afraid the Pollination Pickle isn't getting better – our bees are still in big trouble! What can we do? Has anybody got any ideas?'

Priti is nodding. 'Yeah, if we only manage to help a little bit, the little bits might join up into something big!'

'How about a competition?' Mrs Gashkori suggests. 'It would encourage children to read about bees and think of ways to protect them.'

'Cool!' Priti says. 'Mel and I will design a poster for it!'

I love it when Priti volunteers us for stuff. Best friends can do that sort of thing.

I check my notes. 'The second thing is – well, I think we need to keep our beehives a secret.'

'Ah, yes.' Mrs Gashkori nods.

'The price of honey has gone crazy!' I continue. 'Mum told me about hive robbers in nearby towns. She says it won't be long before they strike here.'

William Tenby-Brown looks worried. 'We can't fight robbers!' he gasps.

12

'Of course not,' I say. 'But we don't want everybody to know where our bees are.'

'Careless talk costs hives!' Mrs Gashkori exclaims.

'Eh?' William looks puzzled.

'If you're a bee-keeper, don't blab about your bees,' Priti explains.

'Well,' I add, 'it's important to tell everybody how important they are — just don't tell them where your hive is!'

There are murmurs of agreement.

I check my notes again. 'Last on the list is Norman Crudwell . . .'

The murmurs turn into tuts, and eyes are raised to the ceiling as I break the news.

'Norman Crudwell is interested in bees?'
Martha McManus exclaims.

'He probably thinks we sit around eating
honey all day!' Priti says.

Mrs Bottomly seems to agree. 'Yes, I do
worry he might be more interested in honey
than bees, but we don't want to be
discouraging. Perhaps we should have a
little chat with him. What do you think,
Miss Springfield?'

But Miss Springfield isn't listening. She's staring anxiously out the window.

'Miss Springfield?' Mrs Bottomly is concerned.

'Huh? Oh goodness, I'm so sorry, head teacher . . .' Miss Springfield whispers.

'Is something worrying you?' Mrs Bottomly asks.

'Well . . . yes,' Miss Springfield replies.

MINISTRY OF BEES

Dear Miss Springfield

Yours sincerely
Adam Buckfast

Dr Adam Buckfast
Chief Investigator
Ministry of Bees

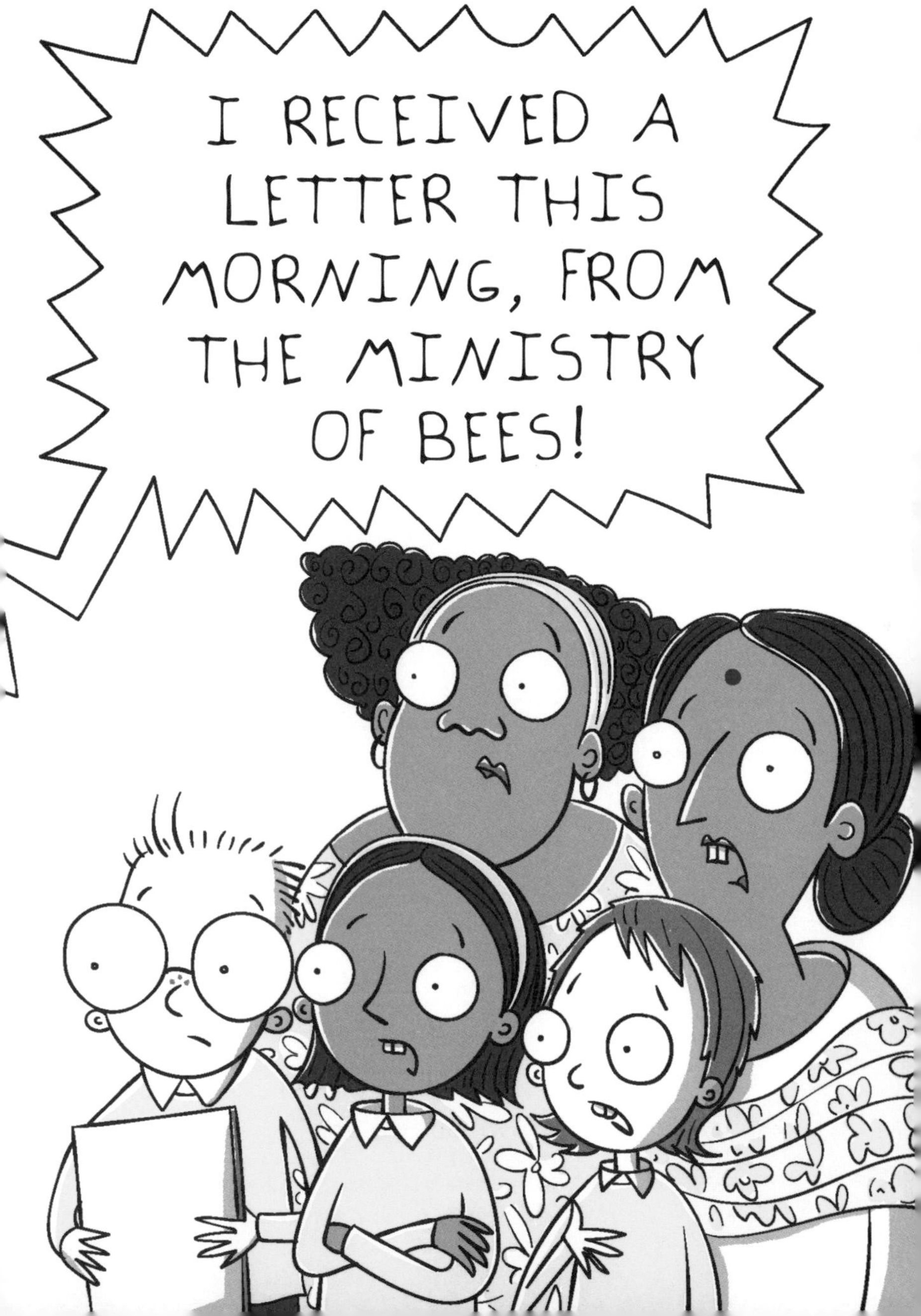
I RECEIVED A LETTER THIS MORNING, FROM THE MINISTRY OF BEES!

There is a collective gasp from our little gathering.

'Are the Hive Checkers coming, Miss?' Priti asks.

'I'm afraid so!' Miss Springfield replies. 'I know I shouldn't worry – I mean, I'm sure my bees are fine – but . . .'

'If they find a single vampire mite, they will take away your hive and you will have to go with them for questioning!' Martha says, jumping up to make her point.

I need to calm things down.

'Yes, thank you, Martha,' I say, motioning for her to sit down.

'Please don't worry, Miss. I know people say the Hive Checkers are strict, but they have an important job to do. Infected hives must be decontaminated, if the curse of the vampire mites is ever going to stop.'

I'm trying to be positive, but Miss Springfield doesn't look happy. When the meeting ends, I ask if there's anything I can do.

'Would you and Priti mind walking Betty for me after school?' she asks. 'I'll be busy with the Hive Checker. It would be such a great help.'

'Of course, Miss!' we reply.

Miss Springfield's cottage is at the bottom of Tunnel Hill. It's a brilliant place to keep bees.

At the bottom of her garden on the other side of the hedge, a carpet of heather stretches up to the top.

Miss Springfield keeps a yellow plastic hive close to the hedge. It looks like an alien spacecraft, but she says modern materials make brilliant beehives. They stay warm in the winter and they're easy to keep clean too. As we approach, the front door of the cottage opens, and Miss Springfield appears with her dog, Betty.

'Melvin! Priti! Thank you so much for coming. The Hive Checker should be . . .'

We hear the crunch of gravel and turn to see a black van pulling up on the drive. A large figure steps out. I'm guessing it's a man, but the black bee-keeper's suit and huge dark glasses make it hard to tell.

Armed with a toolbox and smoker, the Hive Checker crunches his way towards us.

'Right then!' Miss Springfield's smile is replaced with a look of determination. 'Off you go — there might even be a small piece of cake when you return!'

'Would you like us to stay, Miss?' I ask.

23

'Thank you, Melvin, but I'm sure my bees are healthy and there's no need to worry.'

The Hive Checker nods a silent hello as we pass him on the drive. I look back as he shakes hands with Miss Springfield and they disappear indoors.

'Come on then, Betts!' Priti says, lightening the mood. 'Walkies!'

∞∞∞∞∞∞

From a stile in the lane, near to Miss Springfield's cottage, a path winds up and over Tunnel Hill. Betty is a dog with long and powerful legs. She leaps elegantly over the stile and we clamber after her. The sun is shining, and buzzing sounds fill the air. Betty runs in sweeping circles, leaning in as she curves round, like a cyclist on a track. She loves it here and so do I.

Priti is crouching. 'Look at all the heather, and there are SO many bees!'

It's brilliant to see this carpet of wild flowers and Priti's right, there are a lot of bees here, more than I've seen anywhere else since the Pollination Pickle started. Miss Springfield is lucky to live in such a lovely spot.

'Hey, Mel!' Priti says, 'I've had an idea for our competition!'

'Yeah?' I ask.

'We persuade farmers
to grow strips of wild flowers
through their crops – sort of mini
meadows. The bees and butterflies
would love it!'

'But farmers grow crops for money,'
I say. 'Why would they bother?'

'Don't be so negative!' Priti's frowning.
'They'd get lots of pollinating insects to
help their crops, and they could make
footpaths through the wild flower strips.
Think of the lovely walks you could do –
people would pay for that. They could go
bug hunting and wild flower spotting . . .
Think about it!'

Sometimes I wish I were more like Priti.
I shouldn't let the Pollination Pickle get
to me.

We walk
back down the hill,
dreaming of cake and trying
to think of a good name for Priti's
project.

'Paths to Pollination!' I shout, punching
the air, and we laugh all the way to the
stile. It's a good name.

Back at the cottage, the black van has
gone. We knock on the door and wait.
Betty's keen to see her mistress. She
barks and wags her tail, but the door
doesn't open.

Priti and I exchange a glance. 'Let's look round the back,' I suggest. 'She might be down by the hive.'

But there is no hive, and no Miss Springfield either. Betty sniffs a crumpled paper napkin on the bald patch of grass where the beehive used to sit. I pick it up — I hate litterbugs — and I'm just about to stick it in my pocket when I notice a logo printed in the corner.

'T H C — this must stand for The Hive Checker! He's taken Miss Springfield and her hive!'

'Calm down!' says Priti. 'OK, so they must have found vampire mites in Miss Springfield's hive — but they'll help her. It's bad, but it's not the end of the world. She'll be back soon.'

'I guess,' I say. 'But she seemed so sure that her bees were healthy.'

Priti is firm. 'It's like you said, the Hive Checkers have got an important job. You don't want infected hives spreading vampire mites to your bees . . .'

Betty interrupts.

RARF!

'Good girl, Betts!' Priti strokes her head. 'D'you want to come home with me?'

'What about your mum and dad?' I ask, imagining Mum's face if I brought a dog home.

Priti laughs. 'Mum and Dad love dogs, and Mum works from home — it'll be fine, and it's not for long.'

◇◇◇◇◇◇◇

The next day, a supply teacher is standing in for Miss Springfield. He is a big round man with huge glasses and a bald head.

GOOD MORNING, GOOD MORNING! MY NAME IS MR JOLLY AND I AM DELIGHTED TO BE YOUR TEACHER FOR TODAY!

Priti hides her chuckles.
'He sounds like
somebody posh off the
telly,' she whispers,
and I grin back.

We have art on Thursday mornings, so I
ask Mr Jolly if Priti and I can work on
a poster design for our bee competition.

'Certainly, certainly. I am an admirer of the bee and all things honey-related!' Mr Jolly says. 'Let's all design a poster and we'll vote for our favourite!'

It's a fun morning of sketching and colouring. Just before lunch, we pin our posters on the display board to decide which we like best.

Mr Jolly strokes his chin and looks thoughtful.

> Marvellous, marvellous!
> What creative creatures you are.
> I think they're all wonderful
> and I have a suggestion.
> Rather than picking just
> one, let's display the
> whole colourful
> caboodle around
> the school!

I like Mr Jolly.

✦✦✦✦✦✦✦

Since the Pollination Pickle, Thursdays
are the day when Mrs Sweed
experiments with low-cost
food that is high
in protein and
other nutrients.

34

Grasshopper pie and snail crumble are on the menu today, with banana mush for pudding. It is food made from ingredients that don't rely on bees. It is healthy . . . and HORRIBLE!

We sit in silence, chomping on our miserable lunch. Over at the teacher's table, Mrs Bottomly and Mrs Gashkori are setting an example by eating the same disgusting dishes we are. Other teachers nibble timidly from their lunchboxes, unwilling to join the awful experiment. But Mr Jolly is unashamed. He's chuckling to himself as he munches his lunch, and we all agree that it looks totally delicious!

Priti leans over. 'He's got honey sandwiches and honey buns — even honey yoghurts and some sort of honey-coloured drink!' she whispers.

'It must be his birthday,' I splutter. 'Nobody can afford that much honey every day!'

For several minutes, Norman Crudwell has been hovering close to the supply teacher's honey lunch, like an annoying wasp.

Mr Jolly stands. 'Master Crudwell!' he booms. 'Will you please take this honey bun outside to the playground for me?'

Crudwell is startled, but it doesn't stop him from staring longingly at the delicious cake.

'Where shall I put it?' he asks.

IN YOUR MOUTH, LADDY! GO OUTSIDE AND EAT IT, SO I CAN FINISH MY LUNCH IN PEACE!

We burst out laughing, but a little bit of me feels sad too. The window overlooking the playground is framing the little figure of Norman Crudwell stuffing his face. The hunger for sweet things is making people desperate.

After school, we call on my bee-keeper friend, Daisy. Daisy's son, Dan, used to be our neighbour. It was Dan who put the hive on the roof of Meadow Tower and taught me about bees. He's moved away now, so I look after the beehive on my own, but Daisy lives nearby and she's always happy to help. Priti and I want to ask her about the Ministry of Bees and how long Miss Springfield will be there.

We try the front door but, as usual, there's no answer.

'Keep Betty on her lead,' I say, as we walk round the back to find our friend. 'We don't want her chasing Daisy's cat!'

Daisy is usually working in her beautiful back garden. A brick path winds down between flowerbeds and vegetable patches to where Daisy keeps her hives. There are five of them, positioned to greet the morning sun.

But not today.

YIKES! THEY'VE GONE!

'Let's try the house again,' Priti says. We run to the patio windows and knock on the glass.

'Daisy!' I shout. 'Daisy, it's Mel and Priti!'

'I'll call her!' Priti says, tapping her mobile. We hear the phone ringing indoors, but Daisy's not there. Dan bought her a mobile but she keeps it in a drawer with a flat battery, so there's no point in calling it.

The head of an old lady pops up above the fence. 'Can I help?' she asks.

'We're looking for Daisy,' I explain.

'Just a moment,' the neighbour replies, and she shuffles round to join us in the back garden.

'She went off in a black van!' The old lady is shaking. 'I called out – I asked her if everything was OK, and she said not to worry and that she'd be back soon. But I didn't like the look of that bee-keeper in his black suit, so I jotted down his number plate.'

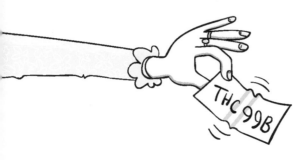

THC 99B

'They've got a personalized number plate,'
I note.

'She's gone with the Hive Checker,' Priti
says sadly.

'But Daisy's the best bee-keeper I know!'
I say. 'If her hives have got vampire
mites, there must be a plague of them
sweeping across town.'

Priti's eyes are as big as DVDs.

⬡⬡⬡⬡⬡⬡

I'm relieved when Priti's phone pings
with a text calling her and Betty home
for their dinner. We often check the bees
together, but this time I think I need to
do it on my own.

Up on the roof, I pull on my bee-keeper's suit
and light the smoker. The wood shavings soon
catch, so I close the top and puff. It isn't
long before thick clouds are filling the air.

I think about my nightmare and shudder.
I would never, EVER tell anybody my
secret, like I did in the dream. Certainly
not Norman Crudwell – not even Mum or
Priti. The bees warned me; they said:

Big troublez if
humanz findz
out, Marzter!

I usually just lift the lid of the hive,
blow some smoke in to calm the bees, and
check that they're OK. But today, it's
hard to explain, but I think my bees
need me. I don't know why.

Are they sick?

Do they . . .

Wait . . .

The smoke — it's
curling around
me . . .

I'm floating down . . .

. . . . It's happening!

43

I land gently in the dark and as my eyes adjust to the new environment, I hear whispers.

He'z arrived!

He'z here!

At lazst!

And then I see them — my friends, the bees.

So they do need my help. When there's trouble in the hive, the smoke does its work and I become . . .

BEE BOY!

A bee steps forward.

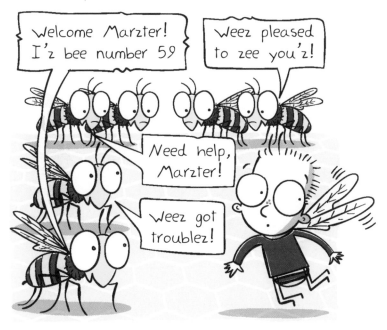

'Trouble?' I ask, looking around.

'Yez,' 59 replies. 'Come wiz uz, Marzter.'

I follow 59 to the hive entrance, where
two bees are holding something round
with pointy legs, beady eyes, and long,
sharp teeth.

A VAMPIRE MITE!

'Guard beez catch it sneaking into hive, Marzter!' 59 says.

The mite hisses angrily and wriggles to break free.

'Is this the only one?' I ask.

'Yez, Marzter. But it tell other mites where weez iz!'

Suddenly the vampire mite breaks free, and in an instant it has scuttled up my leg and sunk its fangs into my body. I drop to my knees in agony, but manage to pull it off.

For a second, we stare at one another, face to face, but with another wriggle the mite shakes itself free. It scuttles to the entrance and looks back.

'Fssssssssss!' it hisses, and disappears.

I follow it outside.
Buzzing in circles, I spot the
little mite scuttling across the
roof, towards Mr Johnson's pots.

Mr Johnson is a friend of
mine. We help each other — my
bees pollinate the vegetables he
grows on the roof and Mr Johnson
keeps an eye on my hive when I'm
at school.

I track the mite, like a police helicopter, and gasp when I see where it's heading. Nestled among Mr Johnson's tomato plants is

ANOTHER BEEHIVE!

I dive to investigate, and land at the hive entrance as the mite scuttles inside. There are no guard bees around, so I follow.

Inside, the busy buzzing of a healthy hive has been replaced with the gentle sound of slurping. A bee crawls out of the shadows, covered in vampire mites.

She struggles to talk.

'Queenz dead . . . weez infezsted. When Queen dies, weez all dies . . . Get out while you'z can!'

I hesitate for only a second and . . .
thwack! They're on me. One, two, three
vampire mites, and they're
fighting for my blood!

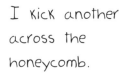

Fsss! Fsss! Fsss! I
pull one off and
jump on it.

I kick another
across the
honeycomb.

But other mites take their place. Fsss!
Fsss! They grab and they chomp at me,
and I start to weaken.

Then suddenly the mites are pulled away. I feel their teeth withdrawing and, staggering to my feet, I see 59 and her comrades battling with my bloodsucking attackers. The brave bees punch and kick their foe into the shadows.

But I'm sure it won't be long before the vampire mites return in force to overpower us. 'Quick, Marzter, weez go!' 59 cries, and I'm carried out into the sunshine and across the roof to our hive.

But before my bees can take me back inside . . .

. . . I turn back into a boy.

My body is throbbing with bites from the mites, but it could have been much worse. My brave bees have saved me!

I run downstairs and knock on the door of flat number thirty-two. We need to act fast.

'Mr Johnson! Mr Johnson!'

The door opens. It looks like Mr Johnson's been having a snooze. He rubs his eyes.

'What's wrong, Mel?' he asks. 'Why the shouting? Are those insect bites?'

I take a deep breath.

'The beehive . . . by your tomato plants . . . you've got . . .'

Mr Johnson holds up his hands. 'Calm down. Yes, it arrived this morning. It belongs to a friend who is working overseas for six months. I offered to look after it — I was hoping you might help me.'

OK, I need to be careful, because I can't tell Mr Johnson how I know about the vampire mites.

'I'd be happy to, Mr Johnson, but . . .'

What can I say? How can I . . .?

'But what?' Mr Johnson asks.

But the hive smells a bit . . . odd, and I've been reading that . . . Well, I'm sorry to say that hives infested with vampire mites are reported to have a strange smell.

'Really? Oh dear!' Mr Johnson is looking anxious.

'It's just that I'm worried about my own hive, Mr Johnson.'

'Yes, of course! We must check it immediately! I'll grab my suit.'

We check inside Mr Johnson's hive, and — surprise, surprise — it is infested with vampire mites.

'Oh dear. This is terrible!' Mr Johnson groans. 'But thank goodness you young people have such sensitive noses — I can't smell a thing!'

Poor Mr Johnson — he's such a kind, honest man. He phones the Ministry of Bees to report the infested hive, while I stick tape over the entrance to keep the mites in.

In less than an hour, the Hive Checker has loaded both the infested hive and Mr Johnson into his van. As he winds down the window to say goodbye, I seize the opportunity and ask Mr Johnson to please find out when Daisy and Miss Springfield are coming home.

We have an emergency Bee Club meeting at school the next day.

'As I understand it,' Mrs Bottomly explains, 'bee-keepers with infected bees have to attend a short course at the Ministry, while their hives are decontaminated.'

'So when is Miss Springfield coming back?' I ask.

'And our friend, Daisy – she's there too!' Priti adds.

'I'm hoping she'll be back with us next week,' Mrs Bottomly replies. 'Perhaps your friend, too. In the meantime, Mr Jolly will continue to help out.'

The lunch bell rings. We make our way to the hall and join the dinner queue. 'None of Mrs Sweed's manky meals today,' I say.

'It's pizza!' Norman Crudwell shrieks, pushing into the queue. 'And what's for pud?'

William Tenby-Brown scans the dishes. 'Dessert, you mean? It's pineapple sponge with custard!'

We choose our meals and take a seat.

'Mind if I join you?' It's Mr Jolly. Without waiting for an answer, he squeezes himself onto a chair and plonks a bag on the table.

'Gosh! What super nosh you've got today — I'll have to make do with my humble packed lunch!' he laughs, tipping another pile of honey sandwiches, buns, and yoghurts onto the table.

Crudwell's eyes almost pop out of his head.

Priti nudges me. 'It looks like you really love honey, Mr Jolly!'

I nudge her back. 'And it's so expensive,' I say.

'Indeed, indeed!' Mr Jolly replies. Then he grins and winks. 'But not too expensive, if you know where to look!'

Priti continues, 'But how can you . . .'

'Now then, now then!' Mr Jolly interrupts, clearly not happy with our interrogation. 'I wonder if you can help me?'

We look at him with anticipation.

'You are perfectly correct to have deduced that I love honey — I'm crazy about it, actually. So I thought it might be a splendid idea to compile a list of all the local bee-keepers.'

'Why?' Priti asks bluntly.

'Er, well . . .' Mr Jolly is looking unusually self-conscious. '. . . for your club — you have a Bee Club, do you not? Perhaps you are all bee-keepers? With the Pollination Pickle taking grip, it would be useful to have a master list of every bee-keeper in the neighbourhood. I'd be happy to . . .'

'Are you paying for this information?' Crudwell butts in.

'Ha ha! Well, it might be worth a honey bun or two!' Mr Jolly laughs.

'Thanks for the offer,' I say, 'but I think we already know most of the local bee-keepers and . . .'

'Melvin Meadly keeps bees!' Crudwell blurts out. 'And Mrs Gashkori and Mrs Bottomly!'

'Is that so, Norman? How interesting!'

Mr Jolly's face lights up. He hands Crudwell a honey bun and looks across at me. 'Now then, Melvin, please jot down your email and home address in my notepad. You can be first on the list!'

There's something odd
about this. I mean,
Mr Jolly does seem
like a nice man, but
I feel uneasy.
We shouldn't be
blabbing about
our bees – at Bee

Club, we agreed to keep to keep the
whereabouts of our hives private. But
how can I say no to my teacher?

I scribble the information down, then
nudge Priti and we stand to go.

'See you later,' I say, and we disappear
down the corridor to the library.

'That was a bit weird,' Priti says.

'Did you see the logo on the bag he kept
his lunch in?' I ask. 'Do you think that's
where he's buying his honey food?'

'Some kids in the playground were chatting about the Tunnel House Cafe,' Priti says. 'And not just the sandwiches and buns – they sell an amazing fizzy drink too, apparently.'

'I've never heard of the place,' I reply. 'Or their fizzy drink.'

'Never heard of it?' Crudwell has caught up with us. 'Everybody in school knows about the new cafe and its amazing Gigglefizz honey drink. Mr Jolly gets all his stuff there and it's dead cheap – sandwiches, buns, yoghurts, Gigglefizz, the lot! I might be getting a Saturday job. Mr Jolly fixed an interview for me!'

'Well, good for you, Norman!' Priti snaps, and we escape into the library.

Mr Johnson
is watering his
precious tomatoes.

'You're back!' I
gasp. I wasn't
expecting to see
him back on our
rooftop so soon.
'Did you ask
about Miss Springfield and Daisy? What
happened to your friend's hive? What are
the Hive Checkers like?'

Mr Johnson puts his watering can down.

'Come and sit,' he says, moving some seed
trays off a bench. I've never seen Mr
Johnson so excited. 'It was amazing,'
he says. 'The people at the Ministry are
helpful and polite. I learned –'

But I'm only interested in finding out about my friends. I try to interrupt: 'What did —'

Mr Johnson won't be stopped. '— all about the new super queens they've been breeding . . .'

BUT DID YOU —

'. . . TO GET RID OF VAMPIRE MITES FOR EVER! Their super queen bees produce strong workers with tough skin, and blood that's poisonous to mites! I'll get the hive back when my super queen's settled in. By the way, I hope you've checked your hive?'

I nod and try again. 'That sounds brilliant, Mr Johnson, but what about Daisy and Miss Springfield?'

Mr Johnson raises his eyebrows and sucks in through gritted teeth. 'Sorry, well, yes, now that's a bit of an odd one,' he says. 'I did ask — in fact, I insisted that they double check . . .'

'And?' I say.

'Well, perhaps they've moved them to a different department, because the office I visited have no record of Miss Springfield or Daisy!'

As we walk over Tunnel Hill on
Saturday to check out the Tunnel House
Cafe, I tell Priti about Mr Johnson's
visit to the Ministry of Bees.

'It's so weird that they have no record of Daisy or Miss Springfield,' Priti says. 'But how does it connect to the cafe?'

'I'm not sure,' I answer her. 'But I was thinking, the THC 99B number plate on that van at Daisy's, perhaps it didn't belong to the Hive Checkers – maybe THC stands for Tunnel House Cafe!'

'You think they're hive robbers?' Priti gasps. 'No way!'

'Well, they're getting lots of honey from somewhere,' I say. 'And it doesn't mention bee-keeping on their website.'

As we arrive, a yellow van passes, and parks by a black van.

'That black van is like the one at Miss Springfield's!' I say.

'Same make, different number plate,' Priti replies, dismissing my theory and paying more attention to the yellow van. It has a bee logo on the side.

BERNY BOZWORTH'S BEE SUPPLIES
All you need for happy hives!

TN63 PRS

'I thought you said they don't keep bees,' she says, pointing to the logo.

'They might be delivering more honey,' I suggest.

But I'm wrong. A woman in a yellow boiler suit walks round from the driver's cab and slides the side door open. She stacks boxes on a little trolley and heads for the cafe, weaving her way through the outside tables.

'Those boxes are full of bee-keeping equipment!' Priti is surprised. 'Smokers and bee-keeper's suits. What do they need them for if they're not bee-keepers?'

The cafe is very busy.

Looking around for a free table, we spot Norman Crudwell. He sees us and waves. It's unusual for Crudwell to be so friendly.

'I got the job!' he shouts, holding up a tray. Crudwell is wearing a funny little hat and an apron. He shuffles sideways between the tables and joins us.

'I get paid with honey buns and Gigglefizz!' Crudwell laughs, and a bottle slides off his tray. Still half full, it fizzes as it hits the ground, and a pool of golden liquid bubbles out.

OOPS!

Crudwell bends to mop
up the mess, but Betty is
too quick. In seconds, she
has licked it up. Her eyes
bulge wide and her tail is

spinning like a helicopter. Then she's off,
pulling her lead from Priti's hand and
running in circles, barking with joy.

'Ha ha! Your dog's just had a drink of Gigglefizz!' Crudwell sniggers. And then I spot it. The paper napkin Crudwell grabbed to mop up the spill with is the same as the one we found in Miss Springfield's garden.

While Crudwell goes back to work, I grab Betty and we continue our search for a seat.

'That napkin!' Priti says.

'Yeah,' I nod. 'I spotted it, too.'

Two girls offer us their table.

'We're just leaving,' one of them chuckles.

'Hee hee, yeah!' her friend giggles.

We sit and watch as the Tunnel House
Cafe customers munch honey buns and
slurp bottles of golden Gigglefizz.
It seems to do what it says on the
bottle – EVERYBODY'S GIGGLING!

Priti and I spot Mr Jolly at the same
time. I guess we shouldn't be surprised –
Tunnel House Cafe food does seem to be
his main diet.

I've got some questions for him,' Priti says, and she marches off before I can reply.

Mr Jolly is talking to a little old woman. We hear them chatting as we approach.

'. . . don't worry, postal addresses are fine if yer can't get the email,' the old lady says, and hands Mr Jolly a large jar of honey. 'Hee hee! Grand work, James. Now, I must get back to me Fizzbot!' she chuckles, and wanders off.

'Cheery bye, Granny, and thanks!' Mr Jolly calls, then he turns the other way and looks startled to see us standing at his table.

'Priti and Melvin, how lovely to see you!' Mr Jolly's face switches to a grin. He offers us a seat. 'Norman! Two bottles of Gigglefizz, if you please!'

Priti gets straight to the point. 'Is that your granny? Does she run the cafe? Is she a bee-keeper? How come her honey is SO cheap?'

Mr Jolly is looking startled again. 'Ha ha! No, that's Granny Huggins, and yes, she does run the cafe, but ... ha ha ...

Enough of your questions!' A bead of sweat runs down his forehead. 'Anyway, never mind about this place – what a splendid day. And look, a skinny hound. Marvellous! Ha ha!'

Crudwell plonks two bottles of Gigglefizz on the table.

'Excellent. Slurp and be merry!' Mr Jolly chuckles and watches closely as Priti and I take a nervous sip of the fizzy honey drink.

Happiness floods through me – through both of us, it seems. Priti and I stare at each other and burst out laughing.

'Ha ha! Laughter – it's the best medicine in the world!' Mr Jolly announces, and he seems to be right because the three of us chuckle and chat for the next half-hour.

The Great Pollination Pickle and our missing bee-keeper friends have been forgotten — nothing seems to matter. Not until we're halfway home and the fizz-effect has worn off.

'I'm not drinking any more Gigglefizz,' I moan, climbing over a stile. 'It muddles my mind!'

'Well, I'm thinking clearly, now!' Priti replies. 'And we're coming home with more questions than we set off with!'

'Do you think Mr Jolly was giving Granny Huggins his list of bee-keeper's addresses, so she knows where to find beehives?' I ask.

'Maybe,' Priti says. 'And she pays him with honey? That would explain his lunches at school.'

I press the button at a pelican crossing.

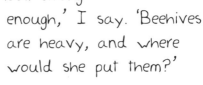

'But she didn't look strong enough,' I say. 'Beehives are heavy, and where would she put them?'

The signal beeps and the man starts walking.

'And the missing bee-keepers!' Priti says.
'There's something going on at the Tunnel
House Cafe, Mel. I'm out tomorrow, so
I won't see you until school on Monday,
but don't wait until then. Talk to your
Mum!'

Last night, I went to bed with a head full of worries, but everything seems clear this morning. Priti's right, something bad's going on at the cafe — but I need to know more before I tell Mum. I munch my boring breakfast and stare out the window, across town to Tunnel Hill. I know what I have to do.

Up on the roof, I light my smoker and enter the hive.

'I come wiz youz, Marzter!' 59 says, when she hears my plan.

We set off across town, flying up and over Tunnel Hill. Down at the cafe, it is busier than ever. The Great Pollination Pickle has cast a shadow of gloom, so people are excited to find such a happy place selling delicious, cheap honey treats.

Buzzing over the chattering crowd sat outside in the sun, I spot Mr Jolly reading the Sunday papers. He is chuckling to himself, with a pile of honey buns on his plate and a big bottle of Gigglefizz to the side.

But 59 and I are more interested in exploring the cafe. We buzz inside.

The Tunnel House Cafe has been built into the entrance of an abandoned railway tunnel. The arched brick ceiling stretches up and over from wall to wall.

Black-and-white photos of
steam trains decorate the walls.

Laughter is at full volume and tears of
joy stream down customer's faces, as
tired waiters struggle to cope with the
desperate demand for Gigglefizz.

Further back, we enter the kitchen. Strips of honey-trap tape hang from the ceiling, covered in dying wasps. They have been lured to a sticky end.

59 is tempted. 'Ooh! Smellz good, Marzter!'

'Keep away from that tape,' I command, 'and follow me!'

It is a hot, steamy, loud kitchen filled with the clank of bottles, the rattle of cutlery, and the shouting of stressed cooks. But above all this noise I hear something else — a strange sound, coming from the next room.

'Gurgling noizez, Marzter!' 59 says, as we fly to investigate.

Next door we find two people – one big, one small. Granny Huggins and a large young man are standing in front of a robot-like machine.

'Wos the problem, then?' Granny asks.

'This ol' Fizzbot ain't makin' Gigglefizz fast enough!' the young man explains.

'Hee hee! You're a good grandson, Wilf, but yer needs to use your noddle!' The old lady cackles. 'Increase the ingredients and turn up the dial!'

'But Gran, it rattles and shakes if I turns it up too much!' Wilf says.

'Don't worry about that,' Granny Huggins laughs. 'The fizzier we makes it, the more we sells! Now, while you're 'ere, I'll show yer 'ow to clean the filters . . .'

While Granny Huggins and Wilf are cleaning the Fizzbot, 59 and I explore further down the tunnel. The next room is an office.

A computer screen lights up the dull room.
'Granny has been typing emails,' I say,
and hover to read the message.

Dear Mr Jenkins

We are writing to all local bee-keepers.
With vampire mite infestations increasing,
the Ministry of Bees is determined to tackle
the problem. You will be receiving a visit
from our Hive Checkers next Wednesday at
15:00. Please be aware that if vampire mites
are discovered, your hive will be taken for
decontamination and you will be asked to
accompany the Hive Checker.

Yours sincerely

Dr Adam Buckfast,
Chief Investigator

MINISTRY OF BEES

'Granny Huggins is pretending to be from the Ministry of Bees!' I gasp.

'Naughty old lady, Marzter!'

TIP TAP!
TIP TAP!

We hear footsteps. Granny Huggins is coming back.

'Time to go!' I say, and off we buzz – past the giant Fizzbot, through the noisy kitchen, over the crowded cafe, and out into the sunshine.

We're just about to head for home when I see a black van parking where the yellow one was yesterday. Crikey! It's parking next to another black van, with the number plate THC 99B.

More evidence. I need to talk to Mum!

I'm back on the roof and I'm a boy again.

I rush downstairs to our flat, and find a note.

Hi Mel,

Exciting news! There's been a delivery of strawberries at the supermarket, so Mr Johnson and I have gone to queue. Hoping to have something tasty for tea!

Love Mum X

Strawberries? Haven't had them for ages. I should be excited, but I'm still buzzing from my spying mission. I go to my room and dive on the bed. While I wait for Mum to get back, I write a list, to get things straight in my head. I think I know what's going on, but I still can't answer the biggest question of all . . .

WHERE ARE THE MISSING BEE-KEEPERS?

'I've got to tell you something, Mum,' I say at tea. 'I think we might need to talk to the police.'

Mum looks up from her bowl of strawberries. 'I am the police!' she laughs. 'What is it, love?'

So I tell her, and once I start I can't stop.

Mr Johnson says the Ministry of Bees didn't know about Daisy or Miss Springfield . . .

That's because the van that took Daisy belongs to the Tunnel House Cafe. Granny Huggins runs the place, and Mr Jolly — he's our supply teacher — has been giving her the addresses of bee-keepers!

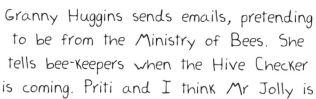

Granny Huggins sends emails, pretending to be from the Ministry of Bees. She tells bee-keepers when the Hive Checker is coming. Priti and I think Mr Jolly is the Hive Checker! We reckon he's stealing the hives and the bee-keepers, and Granny Huggins is paying him with honey!

They must be keeping the hives somewhere, because we saw bee equipment being delivered.

SO THEIR HONEY IS INCREDIBLY CHEAP BECAUSE . . .

IT'S STOLEN!

Mum is stunned into silence as the flood of information soaks in. She is switching from mum-mode to Detective Inspector Meadly-mode, as she pieces the puzzle together.

'Wow!' she says. 'You HAVE been busy. But how do you know Granny Huggins is pretending to be from the Ministry of Bees?'

I hated lying to Mr Johnson and I really don't want to lie to my own mum, but what can I do? It'll give my secret away if I tell her how I know about the fake emails.

Er, well, it was a bit of luck, really. When, er, Priti and I visited the Tunnel House Cafe, Betty ran inside and I had to chase after her. I found her in the office, and that's when I saw the email on the computer.

Mum nods. 'Hmm, and where do you think she's putting the beehives and the missing bee-keepers?'

'I – I don't know,' I say. 'But we must find them.'

Mum shakes her head. I think at first she doesn't believe me, but breathe a sigh of relief when she replies.

I don't want you getting involved any further. This is a job for the police! Don't say anything to anybody. I'll begin investigating it tomorrow morning.

It's Monday and Priti and I are walking to school.

'I told Mum everything,' I tell her. 'She's visiting the cafe today.'

'Woah!' Priti gasps. 'I hope we've got it right.'

'Well, actually, I was going to tell you – I went back to the cafe yesterday, and the van with the THC 99B number plate was parked there!'

'You went back?' Priti looks surprised and a little bit disappointed.

'Well, I guess that's another good clue,' she says.

The fake emails are an even bigger clue, but I can't tell Priti about them, so I shrug my shoulders like it's no big deal. 'Yup, and Mum said we should keep quiet at school, not say anything until she knows what's going on.'

There's a gloomy atmosphere in class. Mrs Bottomly and Mrs Gashkori are not at school today, and Mr Jolly is looking glum.

Priti elbows me gently. 'Both of them are bee-keepers and both are missing!' she whispers.

I'm wondering if anybody's phoned in to say they're sick.

I raise my hand. 'Are they ill, Mr Jolly? When will they be back?' I ask, but Mr Jolly doesn't seem to be listening. He's staring at the floor with a faraway look. Then he wakes up.

'Eh? What's that?' he splutters.

'Do you think the Hive Checker has taken Mrs Bottomly and Mrs Gashkori to the Ministry of Bees?' Priti asks.

Mr Jolly starts to shake.

'I don't know!' he barks. 'Now carry on with your reading!'

But it's hard to concentrate, knowing Mum's at the Tunnel House Cafe while I'm sitting here. Mr Jolly is staring at the floor again, so I scribble a note and pass it to Priti.

But I don't find out about Mum's investigation. She's not there when I get back, and that's unusual because Mum's always at home on Monday afternoons. If there's a problem, she leaves a message. There's a letter on the doormat but no note on the table.

I try her mobile but there's no reply, so I leave a message and open the letter.

MINISTRY OF BEES

Dear Mr Meadly

We are writing to all local bee-keepers. With vampire mite infestations increasing, the Ministry of Bees is determined to tackle the problem. You will be receiving a visit from our Hive Checker next Monday at 16:00. Please be aware that if vampire mites are discovered, your hive will be taken for decontamination and you will be asked to accompany the Hive Checker.

Yours sincerely

Adam Buckfast

Dr Adam Buckfast,
Chief Investigator

This letter's not from the Ministry of Bees, IT'S FROM GRANNY HUGGINS! I read it again to double check. Monday at 16:00?

That's, like . . .

There's a knock at the door. It must be the fake Hive Checker . . . Mr Jolly!

What should I do?

He knocks again, louder this time. I hold my breath and crouch quietly by the door, but just as I pluck up the courage to turn the handle, I hear

KNOCK! KNOCK!

TAP!
TAP!
TAP!

him walk away. Relief floods through me until I hear the tap, tap, tap of shoes. I know that sound.

He's walking up the steps to the roof . . . to my beehive. My fear switches to anger.

GRRR!

I follow quietly. At the top of the steps, the door has been left open. I peer out, careful not to be seen. A large figure dressed in a black bee-keeper's suit is puffing smoke over my bees. He's checking that my hive doesn't have vampire mites BEFORE HE STEALS IT!

I walk towards him. 'Put the smoker down, Mr Jolly, and leave my bees alone!'

He stops and turns but doesn't say a word. Instead, he puffs the smoker furiously and disappears in a white cloud.

I run into the smoke and catch his arm. 'Get away from my bees!' I shout, but the Hive Checker stays silent.

110

Suddenly, two strong hands grab my shoulders and lift me off the ground. I kick hard with both feet.

CRUNCH!

OOF!

We struggle some more, fighting blindly in the fog. But my injured attacker is much stronger — he growls and flings me away. I fall, but don't hit the roof floor. It isn't there . . . .

I'm falling fast, but not as quickly as
the little bee that overtakes me. It's 59!

She whizzes underneath and tries to take
my weight. I'm far too heavy — we're
both going to get squished!

But there's a

FLOOMF!

not a SPLATTT, as the smoke works
its magic and I become a bee.

'Thank you, 59!' I gasp. 'It was so brave of you to try and save me . . .'

'Look, Marzter!' 59 interrupts. 'Bad man wiz beehive!'

Mr Jolly, the fake Hive Checker, is loading my beehive into the back of the  van and shutting the door. We follow as he walks round and jumps in the cab, but the door slams before we can get in.

He's about to reverse out of the parking space, when the side window winds down. This is our chance.

'Follow me!' I say, as a big hairy hand pops out to adjust the mirror.

We fly into the cab and look for somewhere to hide.

'Dark hole, Marzter!' 59 says,
disappearing into Mr Jolly's pocket.
I follow and settle beside her on a soggy
white sheet.

'It'z slimy!' 59 whispers, and that's when
I realize that we're standing on a snotty
hanky. It's a disgusting hiding place,
but we have no choice. I sniff and look
around. A packet of mints! At least they
freshen the air.

The engine coughs into life and we set off.
We can only guess what's happening by
listening. The radio is turned on and we're
treated to the sound of muffled country
music. Mr Jolly likes country music?

We stop, then we start, then we stop
again – is that the beep of a pelican
crossing? Then suddenly, our hiding place
starts shaking . . . .

. . . . and light floods in as a big hairy
hand pushes us out of the way to grab
a mobile phone.

More muffled sounds. What's he saying?

'COULDN'T FIND HIM IN . . .
THE SMOKE . . . LEFT HIM
THERE', OR SOMETHING?

He's talking about me. He doesn't have
a clue that he chucked me off the roof!
What sort of a teacher is he? WHAT
SORT OF A HUMAN BEING?

The van stops and Mr Jolly steps out.
There's the crunch of gravel as he walks
round and slides the side door open. It
sounds like he's lifting my hive and he
must be stronger than he looks because
hives are heavy. I hear a bird singing, but
that's quickly replaced with the sound of
happy chattering, then turning locks, squeaky
hinges, and echoing footsteps. And now
more muffled voices. It's time to escape.

59 and I climb out of the snotty pocket
and find ourselves in a massive room with
a curved ceiling. We buzz up high to get a
good view.

Below us is a busy scene
of stolen beehives and
kidnapped bee-keepers.
Their laughing voices echo
all around.

But why are they so happy?

'Stay here and keep lookout!' I tell 59, and fly down to take a closer look.

I buzz around the bee-keepers, looking for my hive and my friends, but it's hard to see the bee-keepers' faces through the mesh of the hoods. I spot a group standing around a hive and laughing. The beehive is yellow — it's Miss Springfield's. I've found her! And the bee-keepers she's chatting with? Yes, it's Daisy, Mrs Bottomly, Mrs Gashkori, and . . .

'OK, one more swig, and then we must get back to work,' Miss Springfield chuckles.

For a moment, I forget my secret; I even forget that I'm a bee. I buzz close to Mum's hood.

MUM!
IT'S ME –
MEL! MUM!

But she can't hear me – well, she can, but only my annoying buzz.

'Ooh! What's up with this bee?' she says, trying to brush me away.

What about the others? I'm starting to panic. How can I save them if they can't hear me?

'Daisy!' I scream, hovering near her hood. Her eyes focus on me, but she doesn't brush me off. She winks and moves away to a quiet corner.

'Hello, Mel,' she whispers. 'I'm SO pleased to see you!'

'D-D-Daisy?' I splutter. 'Can you hear me?'

'Of course!' she replies. 'I'm a Bee Person!'

A BEE PERSON?

'I know this is a shock,' Daisy whispers, 'but listen carefully, because it won't be long before they notice I'm stood here talking to myself. Yes, I'm a Bee Person, and when I was young I could turn into a bee, just like you. Our job is to

keep our hives safe and help our planet
to stay healthy. There have been Bee
People for thousands of years!'

59 is buzzing around Daisy's head.
'Miztress tellz truth – you'z keep uzz zafe!
Helpz planet!'

'So . . . so I'm . . .'

'Yes, Mel, you are a Bee Person, like me.
I am too old to change into a bee now.
My job is to choose young Bee People –
they must be kind and sensitive nature-
lovers – just like you.'

'But why didn't you tell me?' I ask.

'Our work is secret. There has been no
need to, until now. You are doing a
wonderful job looking after your bees and
telling everybody how important they are –
Dan and I are proud of you –'

127

'D-D-Dan?' I interrupt.

'Yes, Dan is a Bee Person too. He's choosing new Bee Boys and Girls in other countries where bees need help. Dan chose you, Mel!'

It's starting to sink in, I think. Yes, it's crazy but, well, it sort of makes sense. Of course, I know WHAT happens when the smoke wraps around me, but now I also understand WHY!

'Mel, listen: we need to escape from this horrible place. I don't think the Hive Checker is from the Ministry of Bees. Goodness knows why we're being kept here, but we've got to get out! We haven't had any water for days, just some sort of fizzy, honey-flavoured drink. It seems to have kept everybody happy so far, but I'm sick of the stuff. As soon as I stopped drinking it my head started to clear, so I'll try and persuade the others to stop too. I just want to get us all home!'

I decide to tell Daisy about Granny Huggins and the Tunnel House Cafe later. Right now, I have more urgent things on my mind.

'I'll find a way out, Daisy,' I say. 'Then I can get help.'

Daisy points up to a black hole in the ceiling. 'That's how the bees get outside to feed, so that's your way out. Off you go and don't worry, I'll look after your hive!'

'Come, Marzter,' 59 says, 'izz time to go!'

I take a last look down at Mum and the others, before flying up into the black hole. We follow the bright light ahead and pop out into the sunshine. Buzzing in circles, it doesn't take long to work out where we are.

It's Tunnel Hill!

OF COURSE! THE BEEHIVES AND BEE-KEEPERS ARE LOCKED IN THE TUNNEL BEHIND THE CAFE.

'Granny Huggins and Mr Jolly are keeping the bee-keepers happy with Gigglefizz!' I say to 59, as we buzz above Tunnel Hill.

59 agrees. 'Bad drink, Marzter.'

'We must destroy the Fizzbot,' I tell her. 'No Gigglefizz will mean no money for Granny Huggins, and the bee-keepers will be able to think clearly.'

'Needz to ztop laughing, if going to ezcape!' 59 says.

'Let's go!' I cry, and we fly back down to the Tunnel House Cafe.

Nobody notices two little bees buzzing through the cafe to the room where the Fizzbot gurgles.

I grab the dial, but it won't move.

UGGGH!

FIZZ

'Stiff, Marzter!' 59 gasps. 'I helpz!'

59 joins me and together we buzz our wings and push and push and . . .

The Fizzbot rattles and gurgles, and puffs out clouds of smoke.

'Go!' I shout, and we buzz outside as fast as our tiny wings can take us. Hovering by the entrance, we hear a deafening boom from inside — the Fizzbot has exploded!

For a second or two, there is total silence then . . . TOTAL CHAOS!

Panicking customers, cooks, and waiters gasp and scream, as a gush of foaming Gigglefizz bursts out from the cafe.

Food is abandoned, drink spilled, and tables are tipped over in the rush to escape the bubbling wave. Cars screech off, cyclists pedal away furiously, and others just run for their lives.

In two minutes the place is abandoned, except for two little bees hovering over the mess.

I've turned back into a boy.

But this only ever happens on top of
Meadow Tower! And then I remember,
my hive isn't up on the roof any more –
it's just a few metres away, in the tunnel.

I'm standing in the sticky mess, wondering
what to do, when two soggy figures
stagger out of the bubbles.

59 is buzzing around my head. 'Granny Hugginz, Marzter!' she says. 'And the bad man!'

I run towards them. 'Open up the tunnel and let them out!' I shout. 'I know what you're up to, Mr Jolly!'

The bee-keeper laughs, unzips his hood, and removes his dark glasses.

'Ha! I ain't no Mr Jolly!' he chortles.

'WILF?' I gasp.

'Ha haa! That's me!' he says, grabbing me by the arms.

'Hee hee! Stick 'im in the van, Wilf!' Granny Huggins orders, and burps loudly.

BURRRP!

'Oops! Pardon me,' she chuckles. 'I've swallowed too much Gigglefizz!'

Then, from across the road we hear a booming voice:

PUT THAT BOY DOWN!

My feet hit the ground and I swivel round. 'Mr Jolly!'

'Don't worry, Melvin!' he says, 'they're not going to get away with this!'

'But, Mr Jolly . . . ' I stutter.

'Hush, dear boy!' he says, and it soon becomes clear that he isn't the bad man that I thought he was.

I've been a fool and I must apologize.

I am a greedy fellow — greedy for honey buns and honey sandwiches and Gigglefizz. And honey is expensive stuff — too costly for a teacher to eat on a daily basis — until one makes friends with Granny Huggins, that is.

Yes, I gave her the addresses of local bee-keepers, but only because I thought she needed new honey suppliers for her busy cafe — I didn't know that instead of buying honey from the bee-keepers,

SHE WAS STEALING THEIR HIVES AND STEALING THEM TOO!

143

Granny Huggins and Wilf stare wide-eyed
at Mr Jolly, then their shoulders droop and
they lower their gaze to the ground.

The Gigglefizz scheme is over and they know it.

'Now tell me where you've hidden the bee-
keepers!' Mr Jolly barks at the old lady.

But I can't wait any longer. 'They're in
the tunnel behind the cafe,
Mr Jolly,' I say.
'And we need to
get them out quickly,
because I think it's
filling up with Gigglefizz!'

8

We stare at the bubbling fizz still gushing from the cafe.

'Is there another entrance?' Mr Jolly asks Granny Huggins.

She shrugs her shoulders and nudges her grandson. 'Give 'em to 'im, Wilf!' she says.

Wilf rummages through his pockets and pulls out a ring with two keys.

'Tis this big key,' he mutters, holding the bigger of the two and offering it to Mr Jolly. 'There be a door over the hill, at the other end of the tunnel.'

Mr Jolly passes the keys to me. 'Go, Melvin!' he says. 'Release the captives! I'll stay here until the constabulary arrive.'

So I run. With 59 close behind
me, I race up the lane, over
the stile, and through the
heather, to the top of
the hill. Up ahead, I
see a girl and a
dog running to
meet me.

'Mel!' Priti shouts. 'Where have you been? We were supposed to meet up!'

Red-faced and out of breath, I rest, with my hands on my knees. 'Sorry!' I gasp. 'Trouble at cafe . . . got key to door at other end of tunnel . . . bee-keepers . . .'

'Rarf!' Betty interrupts. with a muffled bark. She has pushed her head down a big hole. Then she jumps back, still barking, 'Rarf! Rarf! Rarf!'

A thin line of bees emerges from the hole then . . .

VZZZZZ!

. . . A thick swarm bursts out and spirals into the air.
The bees are escaping from the tunnel!
Rarf! Rarf! Rarf!

Priti and I run to the hole and peer
down.

'Hello!' I shout. 'Is anybody there?'

We hear distant voices:

HELP! THE TUNNEL'S FILLING UP WITH FIZZ!

'We're coming!' I yell. 'Don't worry – we've got a key; we'll save you!'

It's not long before we reach the top of Tunnel Hill and we're running down the other side, with a cloud of bees following us.

The path leads down through trees to a little car park. Except for a large machine parked in the shade, the place is empty. On one side of the car park, cut into the slope, an enormous door is covering the entrance of the tunnel.

Streams of fizz are bubbling out from below the door, as I fumble to unlock it with the big key.

'It won't turn!' I yelp, standing back to let Priti have a go. She wiggles the key, takes it out, and shoves it back in again, but it won't turn.

'You've got the wrong key, Mel!' she says, waving it at me.

I crouch down to look through the keyhole. It's dark on the other side. Suddenly, a jet of fizz shoots out and hits me in the face.

'The level is rising!' I shout, wiping my face.

Then I hear the roar of an engine. Looking across the car park, I see Priti driving the huge machine — it's a giant drill on wheels! But how did she . . . of course — the other key! This machine belongs to Wilf and Granny Huggins. It must be what they used to drill down through the hill to make holes for the bees!

VRRRR!

ILVOLIT

Priti has started the drill and she's heading for the door!

The drill corkscrews into the thick wooden door, then Priti drives forward, pulling the door from the tunnel entrance like a cork from a bottle.

I jump back, as a river of Gigglefizz gushes out through the tunnel entrance.

And then we see them! Beehives — fifty or more, floating out of the tunnel — and hanging onto each one is a bee-keeper!

As the flow of Gigglefizz drains away, the bee-keepers climb off their hives. They unzip their hoods, breathe in the fresh air, and soak up the sunshine they've been missing for so long.

Betty is excited to see her owner. She bounds over to Miss Springfield and jumps into her arms.

Mrs Bottomly, Mrs Gashkori, Daisy, and the other bee-keepers hug in celebration of their freedom.

Mum runs over and practically squeezes me to death!

'Mel! Oh love, I've missed you – well, once I stopped drinking that fizzy stuff. You were right about Granny Huggins, you clever boy!'

There's a crackle in her pocket and her radio comes to life. I guess it didn't work underground in the tunnel.

'This is Detective Inspector Meadly, over,' she says into it. The radio crackles a response.

At last! Good to hear from you, D. I. Meadly. You've been out of radio contact for several hours. We had a report from a Mr James Jolly, informing us that he'd apprehended the owners of The Tunnel House Cafe, who had been keeping stolen beehives and bee-keepers in the tunnel . . .

I nod to let Mum know that they've got it right.

'That is correct, over,' Mum replies, and her colleagues respond.

> . . . Unfortunately, the hive robbers have escaped. We arrived to find Mr Jolly wrapped in strips of sticky honey-trap tape and covered in wasp stings. They can't have gone far, because their van was flooded with sticky pop.

'59!' I whisper to the little bee sitting on the end of my nose. 'Find them!' I tell her.

59 flies up to join the other bees and seconds later, the swarm has whizzed up high to scan the landscape below. We watch as they spiral around, then they dive and cluster into the shape of a giant arrow. We shield our eyes from the sun and squint to focus. The arrow is pointing to a figure who seems to be pushing a wheelbarrow.

Mum, Priti, and the rescued bee-keepers stare, open-mouthed.

'Mel, look!' Priti screams. 'The bees — they've found the hive robbers . . . and they're . . . POINTING AT THEM!'

I do my very best to look flabbergasted. A quiet 'Woah!' is all I can manage.

Then Mum takes over.

'Calling all cars!' she says. 'This is D. I. Meadly — take the B17 road to Hammer Hill and follow the large . . . er, black arrow in the sky.'

We watch and wait, then the sound of distant police sirens fills the air, as a line of flashing blue lights catches up with an exhausted Wilf and Granny Huggins, sat in a wheelbarrow.

Mum's radio crackles.

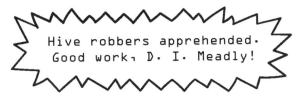

Hive robbers apprehended.
Good work, D. I. Meadly!

Still confused, she looks across and gives Priti and me a shaky thumbs up. 'It's not me you should be thanking,' she says.

Epilogue

All the bee-keepers are safe. Their sticky beehives have been cleaned and the bees returned.

Everybody's happy, and there's so much to celebrate that we're having a barbeque on the roof of Meadow Tower.

Mr Jolly is still dotted with wasp stings. I was wrong about him and feel bad, but he's still smiling.

'The world needs more bee-lovers like you, young Melvin!' he chuckles, munching on his burger. 'And fewer greedy people, like me!'

Mrs Bottomly thinks Priti's Paths to Pollination idea for the competition is excellent.

'We have a spare bit of land at the edge of the school playing fields,' Mrs Bottomly says. 'So we will set an example by planting our own Paths to Pollination wild flower meadow next spring!'

Mr Johnson's beehive has been returned, with a mite-resistant super queen supplied by the Ministry of Bees.

'They're doing good work,' he says. 'The Pollination Pickle won't last for ever!'

Dan's back in town and staying with Daisy for a while. Dan and Mum join Priti and me by the hive.

'You're doing a great job,' Dan says, slapping me on the back.

'Thanks, Dan,' I say. 'I wouldn't have been a bee-keeper if it wasn't for you.'

Dan winks. 'No problem, mate,' he says. 'Us Bee People must stick together!'

Mum gives Dan a friendly nudge and laughs. Priti joins in but her chuckles quickly fade. She looks puzzled, like perhaps we know something she doesn't.

Vampire mites!

Vampire mites are a big problem for bee-keepers.

The real name for this tiny terror is the Varroa mite. Varroa mites feed and breed in the honeycomb cells where the bee larvae are developing into adult honeybees.

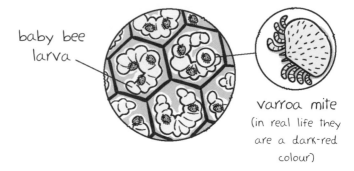

baby bee larva

varroa mite
(in real life they are a dark-red colour)

They suck body juice from the larvae and bees and they spread disease.

Beehives can survive a low infestation of mites, but if varroa mites multiply in huge numbers, they can cause a honeybee colony to collapse and die. Sadly, varroa mites are found in many beehives and bee-keepers struggle to get rid of them. Usually, the best they can do is control varroa with chemical treatments and various other methods.

The Ministry of Bees was invented for the *Curse of the Vampire Mites* story and so was the super queen cure that saves Mr Johnson's hive. Hopefully, in the future, scientists will actually develop a super queen or find another way to stop the deadly varroa mite from infesting and destroying beehives.

Acknowledgements

Thanks to Liz, Gill, Lizzie, Hannah, and Fraser at OUP for their enthusiasm, help, and guidance and for being so lovely to work with. A big thank you to my agent Sarah Such, and, as always, love to my fantastic family for their support. Finally, a pat on the head for Betty who consented with a friendly wag to appear in this book. As agreed in the contract, a box of Bonios will be delivered within 30 days of completion.

About the Author

Tony De Saulles worked as a book designer before turning to illustration and writing. He lives in the countryside and is learning to be a bee-keeper.

Tony has been illustrating Scholastic's best-selling Horrible Science series for 20 years and sold more than ten million copies in over thirty countries.

Bee Boy is his first project with Oxford University Press.

www.tonydesaulles.co.uk

Also available

BEE BOY
Clash of the Killer Queens

Tony De Saulles

'A bee-rilliant read from bee-ginning to end'—NICK SHARRATT

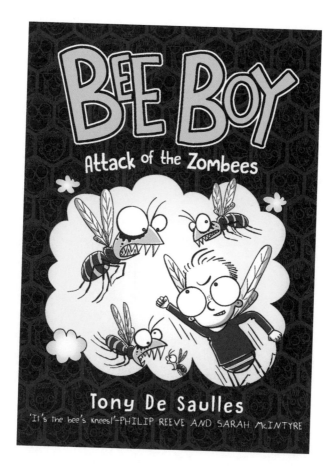

Turn the page to
read an extract

In the middle of the woods behind the factory is a secret field filled with colour.
Flowerz, Marzter!
Just like I told youz!

There is a clearing in the middle of the field, with a black windowless building in the centre.

Rising out of the roof is a control tower with a large sphere three-quarters of the way up. Bee-like drones are taking off from the sphere and spraying the field with a shower of yellow liquid before disappearing back inside to refill. On top of the tower shines a huge sun ball.

Figures in shiny metal bee-keeper suits
are busy on the ground. Some seem to
be mechanics servicing the drones, while
others emerge from the black building with
flowers for planting outside.

We fly down to take a
closer look.

'Building iz greenhouz!' 998
says.

And she's right. It is made from
glass — black on the outside but clear on
the inside, so you can see out but you
can't see in. We buzz closer.

Through the open doors we see giant sun
lamps hanging from the ceiling and pipes
with shower heads for watering. A
shiny-suited bee-keeper hits a big
red button on the wall, and
the plant pots are

sprinkled with the same
yellow liquid as the
flowers outside. There
is movement in the pots.

LOOK!
WEEZ CAN
SEE PLANTZ
GROWING!

Here are some other books that we think you'll love!

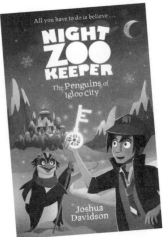